THE WHALES' SONG

To Isha D.S.

To Lin G.B.

PUFFIN PIED PIPER BOOKS
Published by the Penguin Group
Penguin Books USA Inc., 375 Hudson Street, New York, New York, 10014, U.S.A.
Penguin Books Ltd, 27 Wrights Lane, London W8 5TZ, England
Penguin Books Australia Ltd, Ringwood, Victoria, Australia
Penguin Books Canada Ltd, 10 Alcorn Avenue, Toronto, Ontario, Canada M4V 3B2
Penguin Books (N.Z.) Ltd, 182–190 Wairau Road, Auckland 10, New Zealand
Penguin Books Ltd, Registered Offices: Harmondsworth, Middlesex, England

First published in hardcover in the United States 1991
by Dial Books for Young Readers
A Division of Penguin Books USA Inc.

Published in Great Britain by Hutchinson Children's Books
Text copyright © 1990 by Dyan Sheldon
Pictures copyright © 1990 by Gary Blythe
All rights reserved
Library of Congress Catalog Card Number: 90-46722
Printed in Singapore
First Puffin Pied Piper Printing 1997
ISBN 0-14-055997-3
9 10 8

A Pied Piper Book is a registered trademark
of Dial Books for Young Readers,
a division of Penguin Books USA Inc.,
®TM 1,163,686 and ®TM 1,054,312.

THE WHALES' SONG
is also available in hardcover from
Dial Books for Young Readers.

THE WHALES' SONG

by Dyan Sheldon   *paintings by* Gary Blythe

A PUFFIN PIED PIPER

*L*ILLY'S grandmother told her a story.

"Once upon a time," she said, "the ocean was filled with whales. They were as big as the hills. They were as peaceful as the moon. They were the most wondrous creatures you could ever imagine."

*L*ILLY climbed onto
her grandmother's lap.
   "I used to sit at the end
of the pier and listen for
whales," said Lilly's
grandmother. "Sometimes
I'd sit there all day and
all night. Then suddenly
I'd see them coming
toward me from miles away.
They moved through
the water as if they
were dancing."

"*B*UT why did they swim to you, Grandma?" asked Lilly. "How did they know you were there?"

Lilly's grandmother smiled. "Oh, you had to bring them something special. A perfect shell. Or a beautiful stone. And if they liked you, the whales would take your gift and give you something in return."

"WHAT would they give you, Grandma?" asked Lilly. "What did you get from the whales?"

Lilly's grandmother sighed. "Once or twice," she whispered, "once or twice, I heard them sing."

*L*ILLY's great-uncle Frederick stomped into the room. "That's nothing but a silly old tale!" he snapped. "Whales were important for their meat, and for their bones, and for their blubber. If you have to tell Lilly about whales, then tell her something useful. Don't fill her head with nonsense. Singing whales, indeed!"

"*THERE were whales here millions of years before there were ships, or cities, or even cave dwellers,*" *continued Lilly's grandmother. "People used to say they were magical.*"

"*People used to eat them and boil them down for oil!*" *grumbled Lilly's great-uncle Frederick. And he stomped back out of the room.*

*L*ILLY dreamt
about whales.
   In her dreams she
saw them, as large as
mountains and bluer than
the sky. In her dreams she
heard them singing, their
voices like the wind.
In her dreams they leapt
from the water and called
her name.

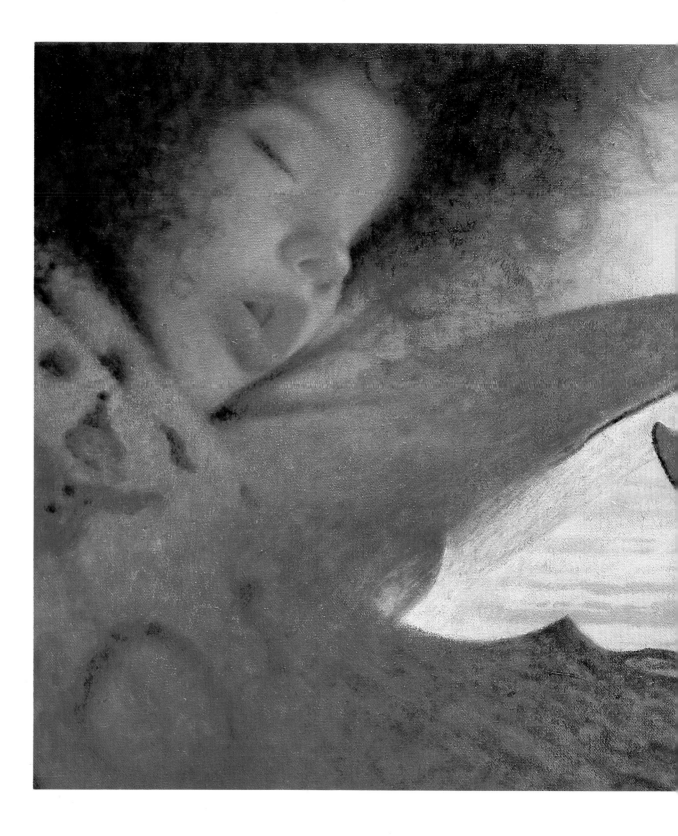

*I*n the morning Lilly went down to the ocean, to the place where no one fished or swam or sailed. She walked to the end of the old pier. The water was empty and still. She took a yellow flower out of her pocket and dropped it in the water.

"This is for you," she called into the air.

*L*ILLY sat at the end of the pier and waited.

She waited all morning and all afternoon.

Then, as dusk began to fall, Uncle Frederick came down the hill after her. "Enough of this foolishness," he said. "Come on home. You can't be dreaming your life away."

*T*HAT night Lilly
awoke suddenly.

The room was bright
with moonlight. She sat
up and listened. The house
was quiet. Lilly climbed
out of bed and went to the
window. She could hear
something in the distance,
on the far side
of the hill.

*S*HE *raced outside
and down to the shore.
Her heart was pounding
as she reached the sea.*

   *There, enormous in the
ocean, were the whales.*

   *They leapt and jumped
and spun across the moon.*

   *Their singing filled
the night.*

   *Lilly saw her yellow
flower dancing on
the spray.*

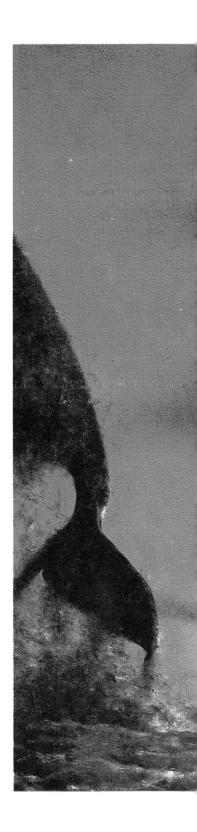

*M*INUTES passed, or
maybe hours. Suddenly
Lilly felt the breeze rustle
her nightgown and the
cold nip at her toes. She
shivered and rubbed her
eyes. Then it seemed the
ocean was still again and
the night dark and silent.

Lilly thought she must
have been dreaming. She
stood up and turned toward
home. Then from far, far
away, on the breath of the
wind, she heard
  "Lilly!
  Lilly!"
The whales were calling
her name.

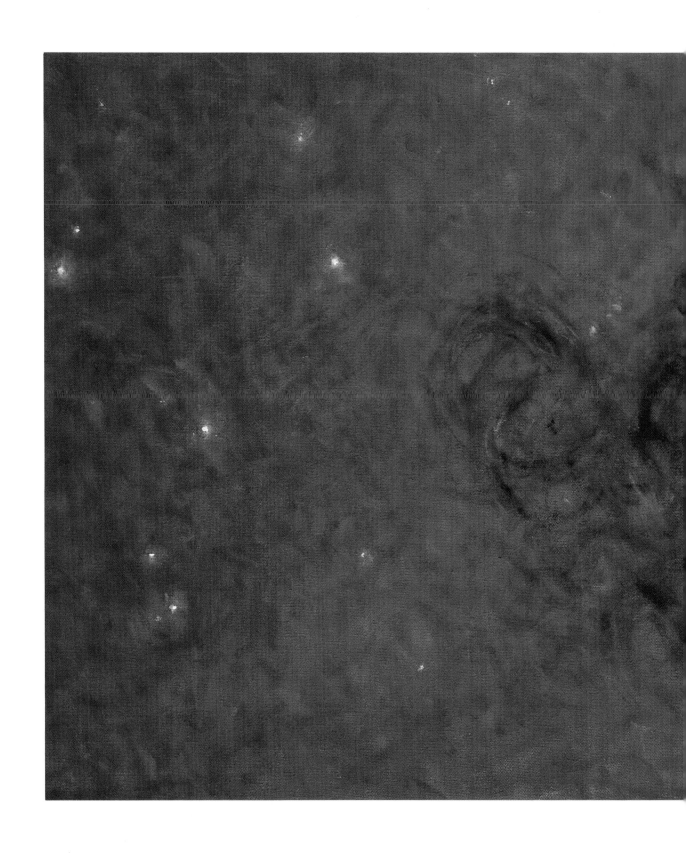

Dyan Sheldon grew up on Long Island, where she often watched schools of porpoise swimming off the shore. As she grew up, she learned that some dolphins and killer whales are made to perform for crowds under less-than-ideal conditions. "I remembered the animals I used to watch from the beach. They were gentle, graceful, and free."

Angry to also learn that thousands of dolphins are killed yearly in the nets of tuna fishermen, she realized all different types of whales are imperiled and began to write *The Whales' Song*. Ms. Sheldon, an editor and author, lives in New York City.

———————

Gary Blythe was born in England in 1959. He studied illustration and graphic design at Liverpool Polytechnic and has worked as an artist since then. Mr. Blythe also collaborated with Ms. Sheldon on another Dial book, *Under the Moon,* which was praised in a starred review by *Publishers Weekly* for its "sonorous text and remarkable oil paintings." He now lives in Liverpool with his wife, who is an art teacher.